Helen Hinsdale Rich

A Dream of the Adirondacks,

And Other Poems

Helen Hinsdale Rich

A Dream of the Adirondacks,
And Other Poems

ISBN/EAN: 9783743464940

Manufactured in Europe, USA, Canada, Australia, Japa

Cover: Foto ©Andreas Hilbeck / pixelio.de

Manufactured and distributed by brebook publishing software (www.brebook.com)

Helen Hinsdale Rich

A Dream of the Adirondacks,

A DREAM

OF

THE ADIRONDACKS

And Other Poems

BY

HELEN HINSDALE RICH

———

G. P. PUTNAM'S SONS
NEW YORK: 27 & 29 WEST 23D ST.
LONDON: 25 HENRIETTA ST., COVENT GARDEN
1884

Press of
G. P. Putnam's Sons
New York

TO THE MEMORY OF

THE GOOD

PETER COOPER

iii

INTRODUCING THE POET.

Helen Hinsdale Rich, the author of these verses, was born in Antwerp, Jefferson County, New York, in 1827, in a log-cabin on the farm cleared by her father, Ira Hinsdale. He was one of the pioneers of that region, and had moved there from Massachusetts but a few years before. It will readily be understood that Helen Hinsdale had small advantage of schooling in her girlhood, and she was married at the age of twenty ; her culture, as it appears in this volume, has been gained by the devotion of hours seized from the engrossing domestic cares of a busy and faithful wife and mother. With these cares, moreover, she has joined for many years an untiring service to her kind by writing and speaking in the causes of temperance, woman's rights, and whatever work appeared to her warm and earnest heart as tending to the betterment of society. She has thus been prominent in the work of the Universalist denomination, and earned a place in the book of "The Working Women of Our Church," published some years ago. Her husband, Mr.

Moses Rich, a manufacturer of Brasher Falls, died recently, and her activities, so long well-known and prized in Northern New York, have been transferred to the West, her present residence being with her married daughter in St. Joseph, Missouri.

As a lecturer, and as a contributor to newspapers of high standing, and to magazines, of essays and stories, but especially of poems, Mrs. Rich has already won a considerable audience, and such appreciative praise as justifies her in this approach to a larger and more critical hearing. This modest volume of verse is to be regarded first as the natural and indeed needful expression of her ardent humanity; it is that vital force that has moved her to verse, just as it has to work. The book is a selection, not a collection; it cannot claim to contain all the best verse of its author; but it does fairly represent a woman's life such as Mrs. Rich's has been and continues to be. The knowledge of the few facts I have mentioned, however, though it will and should contribute to the interest felt by the readers of her verse, is surely no way needed to awaken and to hold that interest.

Mrs. Rich's work possesses a distinct literary quality which entitles her to a place among the minor poets of the country. She does not traverse a wide range; dwells for the most part on home feeling and country life; but she imparts to her chosen themes the poetical charm which every one can recognize, but few can express. Her treatment is simple, but never baldly simple; without any search after originality, she yet attains it by a natural and happy choice of language and rhythm. A fortunate instance of this is the poem "Die, Sweet June," which is a strain of vivid melody, and contains exquisite phrases,—such as "The revelry of golden throats," which brings immediate vision of flashing orioles and echo of bobolinks. Mrs. Rich's sense of the loveliness of earth, keen in all phases, becomes almost passionate for flowers, as in the poems "Death and Roses" and "Naming the Flower." She gives value to the memory of friends and of childhood, and to the emotions of mother-hood rare and even profound expression. What is more true than this poignant thought?—

> "I think the sting of death must be
> Resigning love's sweet mastery;
> To bid our little ones Good-night,
> To turn from home and its delight,—
> Even with all of heaven in sight."

Read, too, her sympathy with mother and weanling in "Forbidden Fruit," and the touching appeal of the unloved child in "Famished." Mrs. Rich writes eloquently on the dignity of labor and the honor of serving our fellows, as the lines to Peter Cooper, to Theodore Parker and Wendell Phillips, on "The Music of Labor," and the vigorous satire of "Wanted, Men" testify. Her narrative poems are on this motive, with the exception of the clever mining-camp story of "Justice in Leadville"—an experiment that Mrs. Rich had as good right to make as John Hay ; and that, as well as the others, is admirably told, with a direct and rapid movement. In a few poems the author exhibits a power of tragic concentration which, oftener used, would have deepened, and changed also, the impression the volume makes. These poems are "North" (whose subject is the suicide of a young poet), "Lost," and "Two Little Graves." It is, perhaps, as well that Mrs. Rich has not indulged in this vein, for of tragedy there are many morbid hymnists, and never too many sweet and natural singers of the holiest affections and the healthiest dispositions of our humanity. Love, labor, hope, and Christian trust are the inspirations of this poet.

CHARLES G. WHITING.

SPRINGFIELD, Mass., *June*, 1884.

CONTENTS.

A DREAM OF THE ADIRONDACKS.

O mystic mountains ! sleeping in tne dim
   Celestial blue of yonder throbbing haze,
Purpling horizon's cloud-caressing rim,
   Fading to mist before my yearning gaze,
Speak to my spirit of your beauty wild ;
   Waft me the sighs of piney monarchs old ;
Whisper your legends never yet defiled
   By breath of fashion or debasing gold.

Tell me bold deeds of huntsmen, brave and grim ;
   Stout Hiawathas, in the deadly strife
Of love with famine, till my eyelids swim,
   And soul stands quivering 'mid the woes of life,

I

Sick of the shallow nothingness that fills
  The idle sails of folly's airy bark,
Pleading for nature, and for truth that thrills
  The brain with fire from its immortal spark.

Chant me, ye breezes, as those torrents hymn
  Sublimest praises to the Father there,—
While the rich blossoms fairy lakes shall limn,
  Angels may stir with breath of holy prayer.
Waft me the incense hoarded in the cells
  Of saintly lilies, as the Aves float
From glens responsive to the song that swells
  From shining waters or some bird's soft throat.

Snow-lighted mountain, somewhere in the rift
  Of splintered gorge, or on thy summit calm,
In elfin grotto, holdest thou the gift
  Of perfect rest, of sorrow's precious balm?
Within the silence of thy columned fane,
  Deep in thy sylvan solitude, there lies

A charm to bring forgetfulness of pain,

    And sleep serene to weary, waiting eyes ;

Where some fierce titan, smitten from his throne,

    The sceptred king of all the mountain world,

Crushed in the conflict, maketh saddest moan

    Beneath the wreck of granite masses hurled ;

Or, poised in heaven, above the eaglet's scream,

    To trace the rivers, faint as silver bars ;

Of life beyond to ponder and to dream ;

    At night to feel the heart-beat of the stars ;

To stand supreme upon the sovran rock

    Where Alpine flowers bedeck the brow of storm ;

To smile exultingly above the shock

    Of thunders terrible, in dusky form ;

To hold high converse with primeval things ;

    Alone with awful mysteries, to press

The pulse of centuries ; to fold the wings

    Of restless thought in heavenly blissfulness.

Never to thee, thou white and peerless thing,

  Whose golden heart the crystal waters lave,

The hot, fierce breath of monster steam shall bring

  Destroying whisper where thy banners wave.

O gorgeous linden ! golden to the tips

  Of leaves that flutter in the azure tide,

No murky shadows on the breast that dips

  The cloud with songful joyousness and pride.

Forever barred, ye flaunting, soulless forms,

  Shaming our nature with the sickly growth

Of all that braves the bitter, biting storms

  Of Fortune,—victims of consuming sloth.

Never the drawling lisp, the brainless speech,

  The laugh unmeaning, the envenomed shaft

Of slander to those fair abodes shall reach,

  Nor shrewd diplomacy employ his craft.

Hoar Adirondacks ! sentinels to me,

  Guarding the realm of poesy, where lies

The pure, the beautiful, the grandly free !
   The slumbering heart of Nature prophesies
Of Time's fulfilment of man's broader life,
   The unstirred depths of being, love divine
O'ermastering selfishness and deathful strife,
   Mind's own enchanted and enchanting clime.

Thanks to His power, the weird and dusky fells,
   Heights still unclimbed the tangled ivies drape,
Shield the great oracle that yet repels
   All that the world's weak vanities would ape,—
One sacred shelter from the rushing mart,
   One august temple consecrate to Him
Before whose majesty the human heart
   Trembles to see earth's pageantry wax dim.

Within these shades the poet yet to be,
   Some bard, like Avon's swan, divinely fraught,
Probing thy secrets, rock and shell and tree,
   All the sweet wisdom science vainly taught

To his clear vision gloriously revealed ;

   His harp repeats the melodies that stir

The myriad forms of loveliness that yield

   Supreme delight to reverent worshiper.

In the far ages hence—the peaceful days

   Of men who reach the stature like to His,

And walk secure in God's illumined ways,

   While all love prayed and sighed for surely is—

This our Arcadia, fresh and green as first

   In the creation's glad, effulgent morn,

Its crowning peaks in lofty splendor burst,

   And all of vast sublimity was born.

MAY SONG.

Let me see ! It was May, for an oriole came,

　With its crest of vermilion and jet,

Darting down like an arrow of radiant flame,

　In a song I shall never forget ;

And flooding the air with a melody wild,

　Half sorrow, half passion, and pain.

The years faded slowly ; I stood there a child,

　With a child's holy rapture again.

Ah, yes, it was May ; for the violets blue

　That I crushed in my palms in my glee,

With gentle reproach, shedding tear-drops of dew,

　Found pity and refuge with thee ;

7

It was May in the valley, on meadow and hill,
 And you kissed me, you know, by the birch
That stands by the little, wild, frolicsome rill,
 Where the robins come always to perch.

It was May in my heart, every folding and cell
 In imperial purple (all sovereigns may wear) ;
May danced in my eyes that reflected so well
 Thy face lighting up all the beautiful there ;
It was May ! It was May ! for you said with a sigh .
 " I love you ; remember it ages to come ;
It will never be May to me more, if you fly,
 Then hasten to tell me you pine for your home."

THE BOY'S KISS.

Sitting by a princely child
Never yet by sin defiled,
Gazing in his fearless eyes,
Who shall picture my surprise ?

When I stroked his bonnie hair,
And his forehead smooth and fair,
Drawing to his lips my hand,
Like a knight of Holy Land,

As the touch of roses pressed
To a sleeping baby's breast,
On my soul I felt a kiss,—
Match me lady's boon like this !

Never ring shall take the place
Of this tender kiss of grace ;
Other lips may never dare
Find the secret nestled there.

Darling boy, the twilight dies
Softer for thy loving eyes ;
Not a path thy feet have trod
But shall wear a greener sod.

And thy laughter, glad and low,
Lingers where sweet roses grow ;
All the world has something yet
Of the kiss I ne'er forget,—

Like the subtle perfume shed
From the dust of lilies dead
Some dear hand in mute caress
Gave to love and—silentness.

DIE, SWEET JUNE.

Ring all thy lily bells, thy royal colors fly,

    Sweet June, and die !

The burden of her flowery state she bore,

    Till heart could bear no more

The revelry of golden throats, perfumes

    Of all the dear, dead Junes.

The phantom rose-leaves drifting faint and wan,

    Slow fading in the sun,

Remembered kisses by the pansy bed,

    Vows that were said,

Soft dreaming eyes of loved ones passed away

    Haunt the still day.

The vanished sighs, the thrilling touch of hands,

    In death's far lands.

All the impassioned loveliness that smiled
> On thee, fair child.

Oh ! rose-crowned daughter of a deathless sire,
> Too fierce the fire

That poured its amber tide along thy veins;
> Too strong the chains

That bound thy spirit to the unburied past :
> Peace, June, at last !

LITTLE WOUNDS.

You hurt me, child ! Nay, it was not the point

Of the bright dagger with the gleaming hilt

Of pearls and turquoise looping up the mass

Of braided splendor, your dark chestnut hair ;

Nor yet the bunch of roses at your belt,

That well might hide a thorn.   Alack !

You pierced my bosom with your softest smile,

And turned the weapon in the aching wound

By just an accent of your dainty French

I toiled to give you, writing half the night.

Ah, well ! girls never feel the stabs they give,

Whilst they are girls.   *   *   *

Grand lovers push us from our darling's heart ;

And when the little hands that plead for us

13

Are tugging at the old home memories,

And urging our lost claims with cooing sweet,

Until they stir Love's fountain to its depths,

Then crying : " Mother, mother, *now* I know ! "

Alas, the pity ! but we cannot hear,

For mother robins singing over us.

MORNING AND EVENING GLORIES.

All my sweet trumpeters, the Morning Glories,
  With pallid lips are lying chill and wan ;
The brilliant troop that clambered to the stories
  Nearest the clouds, and heralded the sun.

I count my dear departed, with misgiving
  That nevermore their splendors I shall know,—
My frail glad beauties, fairest of all living,
  With Tyrian dyes, or whiter than the snow !

From dawn to eve I dwelt among the shadows,
  But when red sunset streamed on pane and vase,
The Evening Glory, white as ermined meadows,
  Burst forth in regal loveliness and grace.

O robes of samite ! breath of lilies lying
  Faint with excess of sweetness, where the sun
Smiles first and longest ! Faith's pure signal flying,
  That morning's loss the starry night has won !

15

IN THE HAMMOCK.

Swayed like a sleeping flower, young Ione lies ;
The golden stream of ringlets overflows
The silken net of lavender and pearl ;
The palm of one enchanting passive hand,
Like rose upturned to meet entreating gaze
Of yon red star, rests at the hammock's edge ;
The dainty model of a perfect foot,
Like lily dropped amid the jasmine bloom,
Beats the soft measure of a dreaming dance ;
The cheek that blushes for its loveliness
Dimples the satin pillow wooingly ;
Smiles break like sunshine on a hill's fair side,
And should she weep, the bending skies would seem
To rain bright gems that purchase as they fall
The hearts of mortals.   Ah ! her lovely eyes

Have drunk the sweetness of the twilight hour,

And droop like pansies, burthened with the dew ;

The perfumed breath just stirs the fleecy lace

Upon her bosom, as a white cloud drifts

Before the orbèd blossom of the night ;

Adoring winds, on poised, expectant wing,

Between their kisses whisper : Love doth sleep.

MY LOTUS FLOWER.

One sang within her ivied bower:
  The summer dies, the summer dies;
I held it to my happy breast,
I laid me in its arms of rest,
  I drank the light of dreamy eyes;
And see! I clasp the lotus flower,—
Star of the East, pale lotus flower.

O strange, beguiling, mystic power
  Of flowers that chained my being; lo!
Where dwells the spirit of the rose,
And the lost violets repose,
  Where the pure souls of lilies go,
I float with thee, my lotus flower,—
Down Niles of sleep, my lotus flower.

18

O saddest, sweetest, parting hour !

  Haste not, my summer, to the past !

Thy airs blew all from angel lands,

Love kept them warm in rosy hands,

  And kissed them first and last,

Then left me but this lotus flower,—

This fair and potent lotus flower.

Dear summer, pass in pearly showers,

  In rainbow mist of tears,

For nevermore will mignonette

Be fraught with such divine regret,

  In all the coming years,

As dwells with thee, my lotus flower,—

Sad Egypt's boon, the lotus flower.

MY OLD HOME.

It stands upon a sunny slope,
   And fronts the beechy hollow
Where glossy vines have ample scope
   The wanton brook to follow ;
Witch-hazels drop their magic wands
   In search of golden treasure ;
And, lying in the silent ponds,
   The trout find quiet pleasure.

The oxen turn their patient eyes
   Upon me ; the bay filly
Neighs softly in her glad surprise ;
   The tender lambs are chilly,
And nestle in my apron wide ;
   The apple blooms are sifting

In eddies on the laughing tide,

To yonder river drifting.

The snowy dogwood stars the copse,

Ferns nod in fronded beauty,

The violet has modest hopes

To pay her fragrant duty,

The arum darts a mottled tongue

To Indian-pipe, and vying

With every flower the muse has sung

Arbutus pale is sighing.

Where poplar flaunts, in changing vest,

Upon my leafy pillow,

I found the child's enchanted rest

Beneath a swaying willow.

What mailèd knights and minstrels old

Defiled by ledge and fallows !

Or loomed against the cloud of gold

That dyed the limpid shallows

And lit, with fitful, lurid glow,

The windows quaint and narrow

Of visioned tower ; the stream below

Was broadened to the Yarrow ;

And castled crag with haunted spring,

The primrose downs of Surrey ;

White-plumèd courtiers to the king

In smiling homage hurry.

What islands gemmed the dimpled seas !

What mountains, lost in azure !

Tall obelisks from stately trees

Took form and lofty measure ;

And cavaliers, with snowy steeds,

Rode forth on errands holy,

While saints, with crowns of gentle deeds,

Walked meekly by the lowly.

Beyond the purple, misty glen,

Among the ghostly birches,

Were kneeling pallid martyr men,
   Whose blood has fed the churches.
The wild rose and the celandine,
   The iris, oak, and laurel,
Were each memento, type, and sign
   Of legend, song, or quarrel.

My world was wide and passing fair,
   The poet always teacher,
Kind Nature for me everywhere
   Was oracle and preacher.
Yet in the farm-house, large and gray,
   The real world of labor,
I trod the prosy, busy way,
   And loved my boyish neighbor.

Oh ! home with plenty at the board,
   With blazing hearth, and mother
To spread the luscious dainties stored—
   What child hath found another

To knot a ribbon, smooth a curl,
　　Prepare a roast or truffle—
To sing and dance like any girl,
　　Group flowers, or flute a ruffle ?

What loads of belles and beaux from town
　　With flute and horn and viol !
What cake, with apples red and brown,
　　That never knew denial !
And father, younger than the boys,
　　Our prince of song and story—
Ah ! well, the dear old-fashioned joys
　　Were more to me than glory.

The household graves lie all along
　　The school-house path ; to-morrow
We lay, with chant and robins' song,
　　The silvered locks of sorrow
Beside the pure and patient wife,
　　The mother loved and loving,—

Sweet death, that stilleth human strife,

    Our Father's mercy proving.

My childhood's home ! in other lands,

    In other worlds will linger

Upon my soul the clasp of hands

    Death touched with icy finger.

The early loved—the lovely dead !

    God grant me happy waking,

To hear again the words they said

    When heart was nigh to breaking.

PANSIES.

Oh, purple hearts that drank the wine
    Of royal sunsets, where the sea
Laves golden sands—the favored clime
    Of flowers—how tenderly
I press your velvet lips to mine ;
    I hail the message that you brought ;
Breathe o'er my soul the mystic sign
    Of Love's unspoken thought !

How many grand processions swept
    Above you, down the western slope ?
How many dewy twilights kept
    Watch o'er his budding hope ?
And did the whispering breezes wait
    To soft caress him as they sped,

Spice-laden, from the Golden Gate,

    To haunt your fairy bed ?

Dear pansies, rich in royal dyes

    And sweet from living near his lips,

Fair mirrors of his azure eyes,

    What can your worth eclipse ?

When, darlings, this true heart shall be

    Silent and cold, to him repeat

My life's unuttered mystery—

    That you have found so sweet.

ONE WHO DIED.

She I have cherished men say is dead ;
  'T was long ago that they told me this,
Grasses grow high o'er the lowly head,
  Dust are the lips I delighted to kiss.
Brown was her hair as the fallow mould,
  White her forehead as marble chill,
Though she left me young, and I fast grow old,
  She I loved—nay, I love her still.

She and I played on the frozen pond,
  Casting two shadows small and coy ;
Seeking for nuts in the woods beyond,
  Sharing their sweetness, sharing all joy.
Berries we found by the ground-bird's nest,
  Lilies we gathered by brooklets wild ;

Ripe berries, red lips, ye are all at rest !

    I am growing old,—was I once a child ?

She and I played on the old gray rock,

    Knelt in the mosses to play at even,

Mended for either the soiled torn frock—

    I am here waiting, she is in heaven.

Well I know that she died not, when

    They put on mourning, I dark woe ;

For when I sleep I 'm a child again,

    And she and I through the old haunts go.

She and I talked when the sunset glow

    Painted our faces with roses sweet ;

With clasping hands, and hearts, I know,

    Pure as the snow from our flying feet.

Talked we of dying, and promised fair,

    That she who lingered should not be lone ;

And now in slumber she meets me there,

    Young as ever, my lost—my own.

She and I slumber ; I awake,

    To marvel that she will wake no more,

For she but now was alive, and spake,

    Calling me dear one, and telling me o'er

All the glad tales of our sinless youth ;

    Telling me tales of the other side,

Where she has waited for me—' tis truth,

    Watching and waiting is she who died.

OLD LETTERS.

There, speak in whispers ; fold me to thy heart,
    Dear love, for I have roamed a weary, weary way ;
Bid my vague terrors with thy kiss depart.
    Oh ! I have been among the dead to-day ;
And like a pilgrim to some martyr's shrine,
    Awed with the memories that crowd my brain,
Fearing my voice, I woo the charm of thine ;
    Tell me thou livest, lovest yet again.

Not among graves, but letters, old and dim,
    Yellow and precious, have I touched the past,
Reverent and prayerful as we chant a hymn
    Among the aisles where saints their shadows cast ;
Reading dear names on faded leaf that here
    Was worn with foldings tremulous and fond,

31

There drowned in plashing of a tender tear,

   Or with death's tremble pointing " the beyond."

And, Love, there came a flutter of white wings—

   A stir of snowy robes from out the deep

Of utter silence, as I read the things

   I smiled to trace before I learned to weep ;

And hands, whose clasp was magic long ago,

   Came soft before me till I yearned to press

Mad kisses on their whiteness—then the woe,

   The sting of death, the chill of nothingness !

One was afar, where golden sands made dim

   The shining steps of the poor trickster, Time ;

And one was lost—Ah ! bitter grief for him

   Who wrecked his manhood in the depths of
      crime !

Another, beautiful as morning's beam

   Flushing the orient, laid meekly down

Among the daisies, dreaming love's glad dream ;

   And one sweet saint now wears a starry crown.

And then there stole delicious odors still

From out those relics of the charmèd past,

Sighs from the lips omnipotent to will

And win rich tribute to the very last ;

But death, or change, had been among my flowers,

And all their bloom had faded, so that I

Yield my sad thoughts to the compelling powers

Of the bright soul I worship till I die.

Nay, never doubt me, for, by love's divine

And tearful past, I know my future thine.

HOME-LIGHT.

When I came with a sense of ecstatic delight,

Into my home from the world and the night,

Into its quiet, love's burthens to bear—

The incense of worship pervading its air,—

The sweet dews of welcome baptized my sad lips,

As a bird in the fountain the weary wing dips.

The soul like a monarch embracing its throne

Would bask in content on the bosom of home.

Little hands of caressing, eyes dusky and clear,

That mirrored the thoughts unacquainted with fear ;

Budding roses, red lips, lifted eagerly up,—

How I drained the rich wine of that God-given cup !

Tired fingers enclasped by the ringlets of gold,

That shone with the gems never miser has told.

Ah, shut out the world, with its hearts cold and sere !

For the world of calm peace that awaited me here.

What balm to the spirit ! what respite from pain !

Like the soft summer wind in the hush of the rain ;

Was silence e'er charmed to such tender surprise

By the voice of enchantress—the moonlight that lies

On my books by the window, the hammock, and
    chair ?

Were the stars e'er so near and the flowers so fair ?

What repast so delicious, so dainty ? its grace

Was born of her presence and seen in her face.

O mothers who kneel by your darlings to-night,

Fair angels of home in their raiment of white,

Have pitying thoughts for this mother bereft,

And pray for the home that an angel has left !

Will she come when the roses have burgeoned to
    flame ?

Will she sing the old songs ? Will she smile just
    the same ?

God help us poor women ! in palace or cot,

The light has gone out where the children are not.

THANKSGIVING PHANTOMS.

Thanksgiving in the great house all too still,
  With painful order, haunted, too, you know ;
Over the threshold and the window-sill
  Are lovely phantoms flitting to and fro.

They touch the dear old instrument with art
  That never fails to stir the fount of tears,
To open wide the chambers of the heart,
  And summon back the sweet departed years.

Dead roses bloom, lost birds take up again
  Their music life.   I hear the hum of bees,
Gay childish laughter, talk of merry men,
  The summer rain slow dropping from the trees.

36

Often they sing, this shadow girl and boy !
  Sing the old ballads, " Bonnie Banks of Ayr,"
Or " Annie Laurie," with a simple joy
  Of youth and love o'ermastering despair.

Sing on and on, their beautiful soft eyes
  Wear never meaning that is cold or strange.
Familiar faces give us no surprise !
  Always before me, wherefore any change ?

In the same world, dear Lord ! oh many a year
  Our darlings live to just and noble aims !
Their country ours, strangers to want or fear !
  Brave toilers, free from selfish evil stains !

Thanksgiving ? Yes, that I can garner up
  The precious harvest of glad motherhood.
So full of blessing, this our Father's cup
  O'erflows with tears—for " it is very good."

DEATH AND ROSES.

When I am dead, strew roses o'er me, Sweet—
Great bleeding hearts, roses from head to feet ;
Buds without stint, and leaves as bright and cool
As ferns that nod by lily-haunted pool ;
And let me hold them in these arms, my Own,
So shall I never be again—alone.

How have I loved them ? All the happy days
I walked with life the old and pleasant ways ;
Loved them so well I gave the best to thee.
These, my true loves, broke never faith with me ;
Nay, in their folds I often found the tear
I shed by night, a morning dew-drop clear.

I want them all—my roses of Lorraine,
The wild sweetbrier that blossomed in the lane,

My Bengal beauties, moss-rose, pink and white—

With all their glory it will not be night.

Let lily-bells alone for me be tolled,

And drape the sod with trailing Cloth of Gold.

O peerless darlings of the sun and rain !

When did I seek your velvet lips in vain ?

Your thorns have left no scar upon my heart,

My first, last breath still yours, a very part

Of all my being ; go with me where blows

On Death's white bosom Life's immortal Rose !

CHRISTMAS TRYST.

Whenever the Christmas-tide comes in,
   Come its phantom ships of the long ago,
With furled sails that are white and thin
   As diamond dust of the wind-swept snow ;
And the solemn joy of the voyagers pale,
   The silent ones with the folded hands,
Who one by one in the dark set sail
   For the isles of the unknown Fatherlands.

If they come back from the golden strand
   That sunset floods with the opal's glow,—
Or drift from the Pleiads' lovely band,
   Or the Milky Way, shall we ever know ?
If floating up from the crystal caves
   Where the spoils are strewn of every clime,

Or gliding forth from the mossy graves

   To walk once more in the light of time ?

I always hope that a signal sigh

   May break the hush of my yearnings fond,

That the lost delight of a loving eye

   May pierce the mist of the dim beyond ;

For who may tell if our prayers are heard ?

   And who can feel that our love is vain ?

That the lost deny us a little word,

   A tender touch for our wasting pain ?

And thus the lights of the home burn low ;

   I move with quiet expectant tread

From hearth to window, as mourners go

   To crown with blossoms the sacred dead ;

With here the ivy, and there a rose,

   White chrysanthemum, holly too ;

What if the fingers sweet unclose ?

   That is for mother and this for you.

Hyacinths for the old and sad,

    Violets for the young and gay,

Returning home they will all be glad

    To find it just as they went away.

Surely, our love ever keeps ajar

    The inner door of the heart for those

Who come from the unseen near or far,

    And leave no trace on the Christmas snows.

Baby's chair where the dimpled feet

    Pressed the folds of his grandma's dress,

In the happy place where the children meet—

    He and she—do they love the less?

Nay, for our human ways are best,

    I should grieve if I came too late—

An unexpected, unwelcome guest—

    To my own, but " to stand without and wait."

All that my Father has given to me

    Is mine in the might of unfailing trust

To have and to hold in eternal fee ;

   If I hold to the bond, it is only just

Giving love for love, and I keep the tryst

   With the absent ones, at the Christmas-tide,

As *I* shall turn to the lips I kissed,

   When I recross from the other side.

SILENT MOTHERS.

I wonder, child, if when you cry
To me, in such sore agony
As I moaned " Mother ! " yesterday,
I shall not find some way, some way,
To comfort you, my little May.

If, when you kiss my silent lips
They will not pass from death's eclipse
To whisper of the peace, you know,
That waits where tired mothers go—
Ay, kiss and bless you soft and low.

If my poor children's grief will fail
To stir the white and frosty veil
That hides my secret from their eyes,

Shall I not turn from Paradise,

To still the tempest of their sighs ?

Oh, patient hands, that toil to keep

The wolf at bay while children sleep,

That smooth each flossy tangled tress,

And thrill with mother happiness !

Have they not soon the power to bless ?

I think the sting of death must be

Resigning love's sweet mastery ;

To bid our little ones " Good-night,"

To turn from home and its delight,—

Even with all of heaven in sight.

LOST AND FOUND.

O my lost bird, that sang to me all day !
  Wee bird, that found its voice within my breast,
Trying its pretty wings, has flown away,
  Speeding to palace gardens of the West.—
There, in a lovely cage, with dainty fare,
  Her bright head flashing 'mid the glossy leaves,
With organ trembles, blended song and prayer,
  The old enchantment evermore she weaves.

When morning sunshine dances on the nest
  (White, downy nest, deserted), mute I glide—
My yearning kisses on that shrine are prest,
  And tears are welling in resistless tide.
O new-found nest ! O sunny head that lies
  Surely beneath an angel's brooding wing !

Sings she, in dreams, of weary-waiting eyes?

And blind to half the glory of the spring!

If God cares aught for motherhood, I know,

When Summer lies in Autumn's warm embrace,—

Her dying roses with his lips aglow,—

That I shall look upon my darling's face;

Note the first flutter of the Song astir

In her white throat; and, thrilling in sweet pain,

Find recompense for every grief in her,

And life's lost music live for me again.

———

When the first timid leaf, with many sighs, grew pale,

And shuddering, sought the ivied arbor floor;

When the blue haze, like misty bridal veil,

Draped the far hills and kissed the pebbly shore;

When all my flowers held carnival, and flung

Their perfumed banners to the August air,

My long-lost starling, 'neath the lattice, sung

Of spring-time glory—sung to death grim care.

MY GUESTS.

Gay trumpeters, my morning-glories, haste !
   Crowd the low lattice where my darling lies !
The braided gold of tresses to her waist,
   And peaceful slumber veiling her sweet eyes.

How glows the wedding ring upon her hand !
   A tender dream her lovely lips disclose !
And lo ! a message from the King's fair land,—
   Upon her breast she wears a sleeping rose.

Oh ! mystery and marvel ! Is it life
   That stirs the folds of this transparent veil ?
Divinest clay ! Awake, thou glad young wife !
   Welcome and joy ! my baby mother ! hail !

What heavenly gift is this thou bearest me?

A perfect being—and so pure, I stand

Like Mary, bowed in soft expectancy

And trembling wait the angel's high command.

She moves, she wakes! a new and holy light

Strikes through my heart from her shy, happy

gaze,—

The mother-love that knows no change or blight,

And fadeth not through all the world's dark ways.

And then, with rev'rent touch, as if she stirred

A dreaming cherub from its sacred place,

She lifted up the little drowsy bird

And pressed her fondly to my white wet face,—

Between her kisses and great tears that said

More than all words :—"Thy namesake, mother

mine,"

And stroked her baby's pretty downy head

Like mother-bird with ev'ry winsome sign.

Who said " a woman has outlived her best
   When roses fade and silver threads appear " ?
Who sang her feet have journeyed to the West,
   When second growth of blossoms cluster near?

Hush ! baby dialect ! the mother-tongue !
   Set to old music—(sweeter for the breaks);
So young these two—the dear old world is young,
   And sorrow wears a garland for their sakes.

Now, like the flowers that open to the morn,
   My life takes on renewed and royal lease ;
My sun stands still at summer's golden noon,
   For God has sent his messenger of peace.

FORBIDDEN FRUIT.

Like a rose-leaf encircled, lying lightly adrift in the
daisies,

The year-old pet lies famished, denied its delicious
white nectar.

The fountain is troubled ; alas ! the angel of health
has departed.

Poor little nursling ! She sleeps like a lamb by its
mother deserted ;

Tears bead the silk lashes, like dew on the fringe of
the gentian ;

Her breathing is fitful with sighs, yet she dreams of
the fountain forbidden,

The warm pearly stream that she drained in her
sleepy abandon ;

Her little pink toes half apart in her blissful con-
tentment,

Like a rose in soft ermine, the tiny glad hand of the
cherub ;

And questioning, smiling, the eyes of the innocent
creature,

Clear wells that reflected the peace of the beautiful
mother.

Fair as a shell lay the dimpled twin palm, in the
gentle

Caressing white fingers that thrilled with ecstatic
possession

With yielding her life to the helpless young life of
another.

Oh ! mothers who sit in your vestments of lustrous
rich fabrics,

Proud in your art to enchant, with music and science
alluring,

Who know not the natural beneficent joy of your

    sisters—

See! envy this mother, who cries in her anguish :

    " Forgive me,

My birdie, thrust out of thy nest, the sweet bliss of

    thy Eden.

God help us poor mothers! how brief is the

    season of gladness,

The fleeting delight of sustaining the weakling

    dependent ;

How welcome were hunger's fierce torture, if only

    my baby were nourished ! "

A VALENTINE.

TO MY GRANDDAUGHTER.

A valentine true will I send to my lady,
  My lady so small and my lady so young;
In her smiles and her dimples my poor heart is
    giddy,
  As the honey-bee reels where the sweetbrier
    clung.

O baby, you came with the thrushes and linnets,
  The roses and lilies and strawberries red;
You shortened the days into hours and minutes,
  With the measure of love just as high as your
    head.

54

Your hair was the down of the thistle that drifted
   Above the white daisies ; the blue of your eyes
Had stolen the tints of the violets lifted—
   Too pure for the earth, and too meek for the
     skies.

I brought velvet rose leaves and dew-sprinkled
     clover
   To match the soft lips, the fair cheeks of this elf ;
I rifled the forest, searched garden and cover,
   But never a blossom like baby herself.

How danced the sweet tassels of locust above her
   How piped every singer in trellis and tree !
Winds, waves, and the sunbeams ran riot to love
     her—
   My bluebell that swung in the grapevine with me.

The ivy caressed and the clematis crowned her ;
   Her little pink palms made the goldfishes dart

Like flashes of light, and the butterflies round
  her
Seemed only of baby's bright beauty a part.

Not angel or fairy, enchantingly human ;
  Fair graft that retains all the best of our race !
If a rose were a bud, then were baby a woman,
  And the peace of the angels illumines her face.

Through the mist of my tears shine her sweet, sunny
  graces ;
  Little mother, my valentine, sing to her low ;
God's smile will make glad all the beautiful places
  Wherever the feet of my darling shall go.

THANKSGIVING EVE.

The wild winds sport with the snowflakes falling
  Over my graves, and the first hoar frost,
Creeping like death on the panes, recalling
  All that the year and my heart have lost.

Is it winter there that you come to-night, love ?—
  Press to my side from the starbeams cold
In the wide old hall, where the red warm light,
    love,
  Lies like a rose in the curtain's fold ?

Is there thanksgiving, with flowers and chanting
  In our Father's house, where ye all have place ?
It is like you, dear, if but one stands wanting,
  To give of your best with a lover's grace.

I marvel not that our world's sweet fashion

    Of love and pity should draw you, dear ;

Could they see His face, had they lost compassion

    For the souls that faint with their hunger here ?

Only a year ! and my life's calm gloaming

    Darkens to murk.   Is it morn with thee ?

From sun to star, art thou free in roaming—

    To bide with angels, or come to me ?

Have you found the key to the secrets olden,

    That Time and Death in their miser greed

Denied to us in our love-time golden ?—

    Ah ! yours the blessing and mine the need.

The moon glides forth and the Pleiades paling,

    Nigh is morning—I feel the beat

Of the mystic oars—he is softly sailing

    The waves of silence to join the fleet.

If their voyage is long, if they touch in passing

    The rings of Saturn, or round the isles

Of the pearly sea, never world surpassing

    The earth they left where the home-light smiles.

And my tears that channel the frosted casement

    Are drops of balm, for at last I see,

Through loss and anguish or sad abasement,

    We cannot drift from our own and Thee.

FAMISHED.

If only mothers knew, she said,
    How hungry children are for love,
Above each little virgin bed
    A mother's lips would surely prove
How sweet are kisses that are given
Between a rosy mouth and heaven.

If only my mamma would kneel,
    As your dear mother, every night,
Beside her little girl, to feel
    If all the wraps are folded tight,
And hold my hands, her elbow fair
Between my cheek and her soft hair,—

And looking in my dreaming eyes

   As if she saw some loving thing,

And smiling in such fond surprise

   On all my hopes of life, that spring

Like flowers beneath her tender gaze,—

I could not stray in evil ways.

I would not wound the gentle breast

   That held me warm within its fold ;

My mother's love would still be best,

   However sad, or plain, or old :

And even though the world forsake,

I 'd love her for her love's dear sake.

CHRISTMAS EVE.

I have garnished the house for Christmas,
  With its holly and mistletoe ;
The tables are piled with dainties,
  And I sit by the hearth's red glow,
Watching my children's faces
  From panel and vase and frame,
In babyhood, youth, and marriage,
  With never a thought of blame.

Gone ! one in a far-off city
  Will dream of his home to-night ;
And one in her bridal chamber
  Caresses my roses white ;
And one in " the better country,"
  Fairest and first, I know

Is " about the Father's business,"—
  Yet their dear forms come and go.

I have knelt by the love-worn cradle—
  Aye, wept by the empty nest
Of my birds flown high as heaven,
  Or lost in the great, glad West.
And I string on a girl's bright ribbon
  (Blue as my darling's eyes)
Some relics a mother treasures
  Of her by-gone paradise.

Pink mite of a baby stocking,
  The little feet, tired to death
At the end of a day's sweet journey,
  (Finding the angel's path,)
Return nevermore to mamma,
  They keep in the walks of light,
And I know it is well with the baby,
  While I pray for the rest to-night.

Next, the glove of a college stripling ;

Then slipper as white and small

As the foot of the blushing fairy

I dressed for her birth-night ball.

She is standing there still in the moonlight,

Love's dawn in her smile's sweet stress,

And again in my heart the anguish

Of the loss I would not confess.

Will my boy come not with the morning,

His proud eyes soft with tears ?

And his " Mamma, *you 're* my Christmas ! "

Will they never come back—the years

Of innocent mirth and story

Those young hearts held in trust ?

O flowers of their May-time beauty,

Are ye nothing but golden dust ?

ESTRANGED.

I marvel, as I trace the white and arid sands
  Of our divided ways, if, in my eager quest,
  Of truth and beauty, happiness—the best—
Has come to me.   If lingering touch of hands
Loses the old-time thrill in foreign lands,
  If the old pain has died from out thy breast,
  Nor bars the door to every gracious guest
Who comes as bearer of the king's commands.
And oft I marvel, should they go to thee
  Saying : " Thy sometime friend hath journeyed
      far,
  Found her ideals in some lovely star ! "
  If then, e'en then, the tender floods would rise,
And drown the fiery scorn, lost love ! for me,—
  The sad farewell of thy reproachful eyes.

THE LIGHTS OF LYNN.

O gentle friend ! when late I sped
   By Hudson's broad and classic breast
And in its calm, translucent bed
   Beheld the burnished, ruby west,
Drank purest life from purpling hills,
   And music from the piney shore ;
Sang with the crystal, foaming rills,—

   Again with thee I sat once more
Where Ocean, like a wearied king,
   With sunset crown o'er dusky land,
Slept in the night's gold blossoming
   Upon the smooth and gleaming sand ;

And read the rocky wonders piled
   Upon Nahant's historic coast,

With murmured legends, strange and wild,

   Of shipwreck and of lovers lost,

Until I seemed to drift away

   O'er Fancy's amber, dreamy sea—

Beyond the light-house and the bay—

   Where tears and partings may not be.

Recalled to earth by distant chime,

   Again we seek the city's din,

Regretful of that scene sublime,

   We hail the lovely lights of Lynn.

The lovely lights of sea-girt Lynn,

   While floating to that unknown sea !

Becalmed to rest, or pained by sin,

   Or moved by heavenly harmony ;

'Mid all of beauty, aye, of love !

   Proud visions of earth's royal souls !

If pleadingly I look above,

   Or where life's maddening torrent rolls—

Still, like a star that beams to win,

That haunting picture fair I see,

Where, guided by the lights of Lynn,

I drank the twilight hour with thee.

THE CHILD AND THE SOLDIER.

It was a wounded soldier, and he sat

With his starved face averted from the eyes

Scanning his features in the crowded car,—

As if his grimed and tattered garb, dear Heaven !

Were out of keeping with the silken robes

Of the excursionists ;—trying to smile

When happy children talked of fruit and song.

Hunger and pain had hollowed the pale cheek,

And from the midnight of his mournful eyes

A world of anguish strove with manly pride ;

Trembling, the fingers of his one poor arm

Clutched at the Enfield rifle at his side

As if that friend a history could tell

To prove his title to his country's love.

Sudden there sprang a child before his face ;

A winsome baby girl, a very bird

Of song and plumage, gay as May-day flowers,

So beautiful !   The soldier silent gazed

Till the big tears shut out the vision bright.

She held three roses in her dimpled hand—

Three deep red roses, fresh as dewy lips,

That trembled softly, while a great round tear

Coursed its sweet way adown her velvet cheek.

"Soldier : take Ella's roses,—please to take !

Ella loves soldiers.   Mamma, give him wine

And fruit and bread !   Mamma ! "—

                                        A cry,

A low, quick cry, wrung from a brave man's heart,

And the sick soldier, sobbing, murmured "Mine !

My child, my angel !   Oh, my country held

In grateful trust to crown my sad return !

God bless the land that feeds her soldiers' babes,

The while he suffers in a rebel cell !

A hundred arms were not too much to give

For one such hour of rapture ! "

                                    Ah, in vain

The allied forces of earth's tyrannies

To crush a land where scenes like these light up

The awful night of sorrow-breathing war.

While the Republic takes her little ones

In the strong arms of fond maternal love,

Trains the quick mind in wisdom's blessed ways,

She 'll never want for heroes to make good

Her place among the nations.

THE ANGEL IN THE HEART.

The hot sun shone on the yellow ledge,
  Leaving of green grass scarce a trace,
Scorching in wrinkles the fern and sedge,
  But the well at its foot hid its gleaming face.

Cold and pure and far down it lay ;
  Thirsty lips o'er its freshness faint
Turned in bitter reproach away,
  Weary sinner and dying saint.

Hurled o'er the ledge by a giant's strength,
  A grim, gray boulder dropping down,
The waters spring to the brim at length,
  And lo ! with beauty the leaflets crown.

Heavy it lay in the silent well,
    As sorrow lies in a grieving breast ;
But ever after, for cup and bell
    Flowed the rivulet, cool and blest.

The sun and stars in a tender sheen
    Gilded its beauty by day and night,
And 'round its margin in glowing green
    Fringes of mosses with flowers unite.
                    .

Ah me ! The heart is a well-spring fair
    Of purest waters, but buried still ;
God sendeth sorrow and loving care,
    And the angel sings like a laughing rill.

THE ETERNAL PLAN.

When the Eternal Goodness said
   " Let man exist ! " the plan was ripe ;
   He was the fair, the lordly type
Immortal—living, dying, dead.

We cannot die ; we live in all
   The ages past or yet to be ;
   In lives beyond the utmost sea,
In leaves that have their time to fall.

We are of earth, we clasp the stars ;
   Sing with the birds ; our pulses beat
   In time with every rhythm sweet
Of hearts and waves,—no discord jars.

We live in flowers, in mighty thoughts ;

    We have a part in every deed

    Noble and true ; despite of creed

Of heavenly pattern we are wrought.

For God who loves and ever lives

    Pervades all being ; we in Him

    Exist for aye,—if seraphim

Or mortal growth to us He gives.

Else could we feel our brother's wrong

    In lands as far as ship can glide ?

    Or thrill with rapture by the side

Of every nature pure and strong ?

O wondrous being ! heir to all

    Our Father's measureless domain !

    God-centred !—if in bitter pain,

Or throned in glory's banquet-hall !

THE MUSIC OF LABOR.

'Mid click of looms and groaning of wheels,

Buzz of spindles, turning of reels,

Cry of crank, moaning of shaft,

Carding and picking, and various craft,

Roar of water and rush of steam,

In our factory window I sit and dream.

Below me the river, in leap and dash,

Foams in the sunshine's golden flash,

Hurrying on from the gray old mill,

Clasping the island, kissing the hill,

Laughing in rapids rippling fair,

Taking soft pictures here and there.

76

Amber and crimson, dun and brown,

Ha ! how the bright leaves shimmer down ;

Clouds of silver, coming to sleep

On the breast of the river, calm and deep ;

O beautiful autumn ! symbol of life !

After its summer of toil and strife

Cometh the glory of love and truth,

Ripened knowledge and second youth.

Even here, in the temple of toil,

Thought may garner her precious spoil ;

Brain of genius, by day and night,

Wrought in harness of steel as bright

As helmet and cuirass, nobler far,

Heroes of labor's bloodless war !

Groove and pulley and shaft give out

Praise as lofty as martial shout ;

Science and labor, hand-in-hand,

Clothe the naked and bless the land.

Wondrous triumph of patient thought,

Honor the minds that have wisely wrought !

Honor the maiden, honor the man,

True to our Father's righteous plan !

Idler of fashion, slave of pride,

Poor in thy satins, this maid beside !

With hair of sunbeams parted above

Brow of purity, eyes of love,

Hand to labor, and eyes to trace

Poet teachings of wit and grace,

Weaving, perchance, with her goodly tweed

Image of beauty and noble deed ;

Weaving mayhap, in her fresh young life,

Flowers to crown her, woman and wife !

Music of labor, glory of toil !

Beautiful world ! When the cold recoil

Of selfish passions and idle aims

Comes to the soul with angry claims,

Turn to nature for peace, and then

Honor thy God in thy fellow-men.

WANTED, MEN.

The times are mad with a fever taint
    In the very heart of the people ;
Not bereft of priest, or abridged of saint,
    Or beggared of bell and steeple ;
Glutted the market with tract and hymn,
    Tithes and missions and psalters ;
But God's white fire is low and dim,
    In our souls and lives it falters:

We have anise and cummin, spice and myrrh ;
    We have stole and font and chalice,
Cross and cushion for worshipper,
    And unction for lips of malice ;
Nave and chancel, with organs grand ;
    Messiahs (operatic and holy) ;

And vestibules where "the lost" may stand,

With the shivering poor and lowly.

Gorgeous temples of brick and stone,

Gilded and carved and fretted ;

Flowers and vases adorn the " throne,"

And "mourners" (for sins regretted) ;

"Talent" in pulpit at highest price

Breaks "the bread of life" serenely ;

Wealth and fashion, pride and vice,

Tread the velvet aisles how queenly !

Brewers, importers, and jobbers make

Fine pillars for churches of power,

Mild and soft (for subscriptions' sake !)

The lessons they give the hour.

O mouldy legends and iron creeds,

Vain words for the lives that perish,

We want the service of gentle deeds,

Heart-dew, and the arms that cherish !

We want a faith that shall ever keep
    True step with the works of kindness ;
A priest so "high" that his glance will sweep
    Through the mists of our social blindness ;
Not quaking slaves to a council stern,
    But men of a wise endeavor,
Whose love of God and of man shall burn
    In their thoughts and lives forever.

See, Mammon is welcome at every hearth,
    While our Lord is a Sunday caller !
Style and splendor, with lofty birth,
    Make the rights of man look smaller !
Sound and whining or frantic zeal
    Drown the still small voice of duty,
And few are the Christian hearts to feel
    A meek life's chastened beauty.

The age wants men who can front the stars
    With their manhood's gaze undaunted,

And keep white lives from the evil scars

   The world's vile code has granted.

Bold men of brain, in whose veins the blood

   Runs warm with a hero's yearning,

Like the martyred sires who unblenching stood,

   All the tyrants' thunder spurning.

Brave men to question, to think and know,

   To walk with a victor's tread,

Unshamed in detraction's fiery glow,

   If in honor's path they led.

To face a fact, or a blazing gun,

   As calm as death, and true

To the heart their love has divinely won,

   With a siren's host in view ;

Men hard as flint to the tempter's wiles,

   Impregnable as Gibraltar,

Tender, subduing, in love's rare smiles,

   With a faith that may not falter ;

As Lincoln modest, as Paul a king
    Of the mind's august dominion,—
Poet, apostle, the truth to sing,
    And lord of his own opinion.

O thou of Nazareth, pure and mild,—
    Our brother, the type and Saviour !—
Who said : " Become as a little child "
    In trust and in kind behavior ;
Come nearer, dwell in our secret lives,
    To ennoble, to bless, and hallow ;
Sow deep, set free from our fashion gyves,—
    Thou knowest our hearts lie fallow !

We have quenched the fires of the cruel stake,
    We have shivered the axe and fetter ;
Now grant, O Lord ! for thy truth's own sake,
    That we make thy world still better,—
That we love thy little ones, near and far,
    With the heart's supreme emotion,

If in marble halls, or with bolt and bar,

   Humane with a just devotion.

Oh, hear us, Lord, and help us, man,

   To walk in the light of reason ;

To evolve a hope, to devise some plan,

   To crush out our social treason !

Must the beacon flame of the world go out

   In the tempest of sin and sorrow?

Let us put the legions of wrong to rout,

   And conquer a grand to-morrow !

CHICAGO.

Imperial city, rising from the wave

    As erst fair Venus, beautiful as morn !

From thy most utter night, rejoicing, brave,

    Loyal, resplendent as of ocean born !

I greet thy towers, thy palaces of art,

    Imposing domes and vast expanse, with tears,

Thou wondrous centre of the world's great mart,

    Giant of strength and beauty ! Though the years

Have brought thee desolation, yet behold !

    From prairie, lake, and forest, writ in light,

In thunderous vapor, fold on mystic fold,

    I read thy destiny of worth and might.

Heart of a nation, unto man how dear !
    Young, ardent, ah ! thy every pulse doth beat
In time with progress ; not a doubt or fear
    Shadows thy future, glorious, complete.

Here, Douglas of the lion heart, thy hand
    Scattered rich blessings ; here, sweet Pity shed
The balm of succor o'er a bleeding land,
    And our spent armies unto triumph led.

Religion, learning, high inventive art,
    Far-spreading loveliness in flower and tree,—
God's special favor surely hath had part
    To work this marvel of an inland sea.

Soon shall the white sails of old Ocean spread
    Their wings above thee, every nation send
Its banner'd greeting to Chicago, head
    Of commerce, and for aye the exile's friend.

NORTH.

He resteth now,—the lone and weary-hearted !

  Let gentle snow-flakes kiss his weary bed ;

Self-righteous world, the desolate departed

  Is safely sheltered from your crushing tread.

Hurl your anathemas ! judge him who flung

  Life from him like a curse, and unappalled !

Sneer at the lyre, too soon, alas ! unstrung !

  Marvel he sought his Maker's face uncalled !

Uncalled, say ye ?   How know ye that his pillow

  Gave not bright beings to his fancy's eye,

Who beckoned him to dare death's darksome bil-

    low,

  And seek the peace of those who early die ?

Perchance the seraph voice of one who blended

    The woman with the angel o'er the sea

Came whispering, when the day's cold strife was

    ended :

    " Beloved, Heaven is lonely without thee ! "

INVOCATION.

O friend, amid the stately pines
    That murmurous music yield to thee,
Recall'st thou the enchanted climes,
    St. Lawrence broad and clear and free ?
What time we sailed in summer calm,
    With moonlight glinting wave and beach,
To meet the south wind's kiss of balm,
    Surpassing melody of speech ?

At night when the Nevada gleams,
    Like castle turrets, white and cold,
And all the azure archway streams
    With oriflamme of gems and gold ;
Upon thy lonely snow-crowned beat,
    Where foams and falls the mountain rill,

Come visions of our voyages sweet,
　　By sheltered bay and wooded hill ?

And fairy isles that slept serene
　　Upon the river's peaceful breast,
While cloth of gold some naiad queen
　　Trailed regally along the west ;
With furrows left by gliding keel,
　　And lilies clasping to their hearts
The golden secrets stars reveal
　　When rosy Day at length departs ?

Still on and on, as spirits float,
　　Through waves of ether opal-rifted,
Too blest, enrapt, to ever note
　　If down to death we slowly drifted ;
Now sighing faint, with clover gales,
　　Then distant bell rang out delight,
Anon the dusky grotto vales,—
　　A fitting scene for such a night.

Ah ! from thy lips that keep for me

   Poems no bard hath ever sung,

Still falls the entrancing melody

   Of Grecian isles when time was young?

Fair river, clasp unto thy breast

   Our love,—nay, tell it to the main !

Old Ocean, bear it to the West,

   And wake his smile for me again !

IF ONLY.

If only over the wastes of snow
The sweet south wind like a breath would blow,
Soft and fitful, as comes and goes
The breath of my one white folded Rose,
Sleeping to-night in the moonbeams fair,
That touch with blessing her bonnie hair,
Afar where the south-land smiling lies
Under the hyacinth brooding skies,—
The dull, sad ache of my heart would cease
As the spring's warm kiss gives the buds release.

If only a May-bird, brave and free,
Could come on a mission of hope to me,
A wingèd echo of songs that float,

Clear and glad from her dainty throat,

Bringing the charm of my darling's face,

Her clasping arms in a fond embrace,—

The billows of snow on the dreary wold

Would change to meadows of green and gold,

Scent of clover and hum of bees

Drift through the lawn and its stately trees.

The brook that ripples in laughter light

Where the daisy flutters her signal white,

And mottled lilies, like knights of yore

Trailing their banners through gouts of gore,

With plumy ferns where the blue-bells chime

Low to the heart of its love-lit clime,

And all the pomp of the summer thrills

Like a breeze from the sun-kissed, purple hills,

Where the Arno sings to the waiting sea,

As my soul floats out in a psalm to thee.

THINK NOBLE THINGS OF GOD.

If wrong and sorrow compass thee,
Keep step with nature's harmony,
Anon the evil shadows flee.

If, sowing full and precious grain,
The harvest yield thee bitter pain,
Say not that human love is vain.

If earnest eyes of tender trust
Grow cold (as blind with doubt they must),
See that *thou* fail not to be just.

There comes an hour to him, to thee,
When all thy true heart's fealty
Shall dower his soul with purity.

If finding some poor lamb astray
(Even thy foe's) while yet 't is day
Bear it to fold by mercy's way.

If, when the twilight comes to weep,
Thy little summer daisy sleep,
Doubt not that God the germ will keep.

When in the brown and gracious mould
Thy flower lies, from heart of gold
An angel's wings of light unfold.

For "God is God"; whate'er betide,
His love and justice will abide,
And find thee through thy mail of pride.

Though creeds conflict, they do not jar
His purpose—not a flower or star
But smiles from out the smoke of war.

Are we not parts of God ? and lo !
Where'er thou goest He must go,
Even beyond the hills of snow,

From harebell to anemone,
That waves in some fair southern sea,
To worlds that fill immensity,

His universe is not the loom
Where any thread will fail too soon ;
The fair design will bud and bloom.

"Think noble things of God," for then
It follows that thy fellow-men
From thee shall suffer wrong nor pain.

THE ENGINEER'S STORY.

We were buried in the snow-field, in the cañons
   east Pacific,
Short of sunshine, yet the storm-fiend in his bless-
   ings most prolific,
And, between the lack of coal and the scant supply
   of rations,
The terminus seemed nearing without passing any
   stations.

Now, to shoot across the chasms, and to reach the
   grand Sierras,
Where the stars in smoke and vapor seem like
   ruddy, hanging cherries,

With the air like an elixir, is a rapture worthy
   heroes,—

But to starve in prisons, comrades, with the weather
   in the zeroes !

We had toiled like giants, listened for the "fast
   express " with faces

Begrimed, yet white, and not with frost, nor bright
   with Christian graces ;

The hunger and the cold, you see, on railroad men
   are trying,

And the face of honest labor is a poor resort for
   lying.

You can brave a danger coming with a shriek and
   rush and tremble,

Like a roar of bursting bombs,—not Death stooping
   dissemble,

And stealing on you softly, like a great white bear,
to smother

Every manly throb, until you turn aghast from one
another.

God of mercy! that last evening, by our dim fire,
hunger-driven,

Failing succor, only whiskey, failing hope, (and may
be Heaven,)

Can you marvel if we broke the pledge, even passing
it to Brodie?

He struck the flask aside, and groaned : "Not if I
perish, Maudie!

"Don't, boys! see, here are rations ; I have saved
mine for your taking ;

Leave the poison ; I am glad to die, my heart has
long been breaking ;

Eat, while I pray to God, and her, my darling and
   my angel!"
Then we knew our grim old hero was a martyr, an
   evangel.

Were we blind? But woe is selfish, and the
   engineer was dying.
"Nay, my boys, to starve is nothing to remorse
   that's ever sighing.
I used to run the 'lightning' on the Central, and
   the fellows
Always smiled to see me hasten when we came in
   sight of Bellows.

"For my daughter, little Maudie, with her hair like
   sunbeams braided,
And eyes of tender yearning by the white Nor-
   mandy shaded;

Ribbons flying, ringlets dancing, lips aglow with
merry greeting ;
Dimpled arms held out to clasp me ; oh, the bliss
of such a meeting ! "

And the great sad eyes grew misty, like the gloaming by a river ;
And the brown hand sought his bosom in an eager
sort of shiver,—
Found, and kissed a locket meekly with the blanch-
ing lips of famine ;
Showed it us : " My crucifix !—please, boys, no
more of damning."

" Such a beauty !—Is she living?" Poor Jack
Brodie, kneeling, crying :
" Living ? yes, with holy beings !—but I saw my
baby lying

Stark and crushed beneath my engine,—can I ever
  hope to reach her?

Is there expiation, mercy, for a lost, a wretched
  creature?

" I had drank that fatal morning, and a broken rail
  was lying

Near the crossing; she espied it, and with tiny
  lantern flying,

Bravely swung the warning signal.   But my hand,
  alas, unsteady !—

And I staggered, sick with horror, to her little
  mangled body."

He was silent, gasping, shaking, but a cry of anguish
  ringing

Through the car with sobs of pity, and Jack Brodie, kneeling, clinging

To her sweet face within failing sight,—" Don't
　　drink, my boys," he said ;

" I have tried to do a little good, my angel ! "—Jack
　　was dead.

How we knelt and kissed his forehead, kissed her
　　pictured face so fair ;

And we took the pledge forever, in the solemn hush
　　of prayer,

Resolved to die (if die we must) like men, not as
　　the beast,—

And then we heard the " General Grant " come
　　screaming from the East.

JUSTICE IN LEADVILLE.

Yes, law is a great thing, mister, but justice comes
in ahead

When a lie makes a fiend not guilty, and the neighbor he shot is dead.

Leadville would follow the fashion,—have regular
courts of law,—

I take no stock in lawyers, don't gamble upon their
jaw ;

But the judge he said Gueldo undoubtedly did for
Blake,

And we ought to give him a trial, just for appear-
ance' sake ;

That Texas chap can't clear him, the lead 's too
rich to hide,

And the black neck of the Spaniard on the air-line 's
  bound to ride.

So I tried to believe in the woman with the bandage
  upon her eyes,

Though one side 's as likely as t' other to drop from
  the beam or rise

If a nugget should tip the balance or a false tongue
  cry the weight ;

But I thought I 'd see if a trial was " the regular
  thing " for Kate.

So I went to her pretty cottage ; the widow 's a tidy
  thing,—

Great mournful eyes, and a head of hair as brown
  as a heron's wing.

Her husband's murder was cruel ; Antonio, fierce
  and sly,

Had sworn revenge for a trifle when some of the
  boys were nigh.

She had tripped to her bed of pansies, for Blake was
    going away ;

While he bent to embrace their baby she gathered a
    love bokay.

She heard a voice,—Gueldo's,—a shot,—and she
    ran to Jim ;

But the baby's white dress was scarlet, and his
    father's eyes were dim.

You 've heard the cry of a bittern ?—it was just
    that sort of a noise ;

It brought us there in a hurry,—the women and
    half the boys.

She tried to tell us the story,—her white lips only
    stirred ;

She seemed to slip quite out of life, and could n't
    utter a word.

She told us at last in writing, only a name,—and
    then

Six derringers found his level, his guard was a
　　dozen men.

She did n't take on, seemed frozen,—but Lord !
　　what a ghastly face !

With slow, sad steps, like the shade of joy, she crept
　　round the woful place,

And when we lifted the coffin she knelt with her
　　little child,

Just whispered to Jim and kissed him ; we said she
　　was going wild.

Ah ! deep things yield no token, and she wa' n't
　　surface gold ;

'T was a gloomy job prospecting round the claim
　　Jim could n't hold.

But I found her rocking the baby, her chin in the
　　dainty palm,

White as the shaver's pillow, tearless, and dreadful
　　calm.

I told her about the trial ; she shuddered, her great
 black eyes
Flashed out such a danger signal,—or may be it
 was surprise.
" They never can clear Gueldo,—he cannot escape,
 for I
Can swear to his hissing Spanish,—that I saw him
 turn and fly ! "
" No, never," I said ; " his ticket is good for the
 underground ;
He 's due this time to-morrow where he won't find
 Blake around."

The judge held court in his wood-house, and Bagget
 had stripped his store
Of barrel and box ; I never set eyes on a crowd
 before.
I dropped on a keg of ciscos, the judge on a box of
 soap ;
Gueldo and his attorney found seats on a coil of rope.

Then Kate came, with her baby like a rosebud in
    the snow,

Its pink cheek against the mother's pallid and
    pinched with woe.

Jim's blue eyes, as I live, sir ! there were his very
    curls ;

They set us miners to sobbing like a corral of silly
    girls.

She looked so thankful on us, colored, and when
    she met

The snake eyes of Gueldo, the braids on her brow
    were wet ;

And if the hell of the preachers had yawned on our
    gentle Kate,

She could n't have glared such horror or woman's
    deadly hate.

Well, they went on with the trial ; an alibi, it was
    claimed,

Would be urged for the wolf defendant ; the judge,—
    well, he looked ashamed,

When ten of the hardest rascals, the cruellest, mean-
 est lot,

Swore, black and blue, Gueldo was four miles from
 the spot

With them, a-hunting the grizzly ; then the Texan
 pled his case,

Till the judge turned pale as ashes,—could n't look
 in an honest face.

"Your verdict, my men of the jury, must be
 grounded, I suppose,

On the weight of the testimony ; if you have any
 faith in those

Re*li*able fellows from Gouger, the prisoner was not
 thar."

And his honor growled upon him like a vexed and
 and hungry b'ar.

I 've noticed the newest convert prays loudest of all
 the camp ;

And that mutton-headed jury declared for the
cussèd scamp.

For nothing Kate's truthful story; the evidence
went, you see,

To disprove the facts ; Gueldo by the law was ac-
quitted, free.

"You can go," said the judge; "but likely the
climate won't suit you here."

Antonio rose defiant.

Then Kate spoke, low and clear,

(Clasping her babe, and rising,) "Are you done
with the prisoner, sir ? "

As a marble statue might ask it.   His honor bowed
to her,—

"Heaven knows I'm sorry I am, child." "Be-
cause," she replied, " I am not."

A flash from her eyes and pistol,—the Mexican
devil was shot.

The smoke made a little halo round the laughing
baby's head.

Then I knew the terrible promise she whispered
   her husband dead.

Gueldo staggered, falling, his swart face scared and
   grim,—

" Dead, gentlemen of the jury !   Decision reversed
   for him !

And justice !" we heard her murmur, though she ,
   was n't the talking kind,

And she had n't the least allusion to that female
   pictured blind.

Trembling she turned upon us the eyes of a
   wounded doe ;

" Amen !" from the weeping neighbors ; " God
   help you ! " the judge said ; " go ! "

COMPANY K.

Inscribed to its Colonel, Hon. A. G. ——.

Up in the garret, with quaint, dear things—

Baby's crib, where he found his wings,

And floated away from me, fast and far,—

I keep this blood-stained, battered star.

And all that its blue, cold lips can say,

A bullet's inscription, and " Company K."

Under the eaves in the sweet May sun

Swallows are piping, the love task done ;

Robins and lilacs, beauty and sound,

Life is pulsing in all around ;

But through the vista of tears, to-day,

I see them muster our Company K.

113

Just out there, on the village park,

In May-day sunshine they gather—hark !

Mournful drum-beats and bugle's call,

Our boys in blue—I behold them all ;

Stalwart, manly, heroic, gay,—

Strange—there 's but one man of Company K.

One white forehead with locks of dun,

A fond mouth's sweetness (only one),

A long "farewell" in the tender eyes,

A red rose kissed in a rapt surprise,

A gallant salute as he rode away

To death and honor, *my* Company K.

Alas ! why tell of the awful strife,

His battles of death, and my battles of life—

The tiny marvel of love and grace,

That never might look on his father's face,

The blighted bud on my heart that lay

One year from the marching of Company K.

Ah, well ! his letters were " bread and wine "

To lips of famine : he said that mine

" Had baby fingers and eyes " to him,

So dear, all the stars on the flag grew dim

In memory's mist through the deadly fray

That covered with glory brave Company K.

Then came the last ! the despatch had said :

" At Gettysburg the reserve he led ;

(And had he lived,) from our Grant's own hand

A general's brevet of the Army Grand."

But this my darling had strength to say:

" My love, remember ! " and " Company K."

We found the dust of a red rose there,

Just beneath this star, and a tress of hair,

And the golden head of our baby lies

Close to his lips and his brooding eyes,

See ! the sod will break into flowers of May,

Keeping tryst with *my* star of old Company K.

GUESS WHO?

———

I know a little dark-eyed maid,

With hair of ebon-gloss and shade,

With lips of coral, and a grace

In speech, and form, and lovely face;

Ah, one a fairy prince might woo!

                        Guess who?

And oft with such a pensive charm

In those sweet eyes we take alarm,

Lest beings hid from us may stand

And beckon her to angel land ;

I know her name, and so do you !

                        Guess who?

She sings like birds that soaring die,

Such rapt repose in lip and eye !

I watch to see her drift from sight,

Leaving my world in utter night.

She loves me, but she loves not you !

Guess who ?

ONLY A WOMAN.

The heroine of " Long Point Isle," like a schooner's
mast she stands,

With mother-love in smile and voice, if brown her
shapely hands ;

Broad bosomed, large of limb ! blue eyes of clear
and level glance

Look out 'neath brow serene with thoughts of
childhood and of France ;

And when the wild waves rend the dunes, she
dreams of old Marseilles,

For Erie rages like the sea in fierce December
gales.

Hers all a woman's patient trust, a woman's cour-
age fine ;

Her hair like ancient viking's gold, her lips as red
    as wine.

The simple wonder of her gaze, its pathos deep
    inclines

The mind to pictured saints, the dames of Spenser's
    classic lines.

She moves with free, unstudied grace, Juno in
    russet gray !

A noble nature giveth ease, the royal right of way

To every heart, for never soul as white and brave
    was sent

To yearn and strive for broader range, in sickly
    tenement.

Where comes the wild sea-fowl to moult, the mink
    to build her nest,

The antlered deer to drink, where flames the cloud-
    empurpled west ;

Where cedared swamps with ghostly birch and
    mournful sighing pines

Shadow the pools and sand-hills draped with noi-
  some tangled vines.
In trapper's hut, with precious brood, six fair-haired
  sons and daughters,
She dignifies her low estate, this "Lady of the
  Waters."
Did she ponder on the problems that perplex our
  modern thought?
Did she sigh for wealth and glory? Nay; the ser-
  vice that she brought
Was love's unwearied struggle for the timid lambs
  afold,
Unselfish duties meekly done, with spirit strong
  and bold.

The "Conductor," Captain Hackett, sailing west-
  ward for the straits,
Met the demons of the tempest in the seething,
  blackened gates

Where the Lake of Woods is narrowed by the island
and the land.

Frozen spray and shoal around him, terrors dire on
every hand,

And the gallant schooner foundered, like a hunted
stag at bay;

Lashed to icy masts, poor tortured ones, they waited
for the day.

And when it broke in snow and wind, horror fell
upon the men ;

Vain the hope of human succor in the "Devil's
Cut"!   But then—

Was it angel?   Was it woman?   Lo! between the
surges high

And a mighty bonfire blazing, something mortal
draweth nigh !

It is she, the hermit matron.   She has left her little
flock,

Reaching arms of mad entreaty where the freezing
sailors rock

In the creaking shrouds, yet shrinking from the
    yawning grave below.

In vain her "signal service"; still they clung, in
    fear and woe,

Until sunset slowly lifted its black lid in angry fire

On the shipwreck and the woman, on the broad
    and flashing pyre.

Then she cried in anguish : "Father, keep my little
    ones!" and bore

Streaming torch above her, dashing through the surf
    that rent the shore.

There with death the captain battled ; and with
    sinews pity-strung

She snatched him from the undertow ; a giantess,
    she sprung

Up dizzy bank, and laid her prize beside the glow-
    ing coals—

Returned, and, one by one, she saved the six im-
    perilled souls.

"One for every child," she murmured ; "life for

life ! bless God !" and went

To her round of quiet duties, singing in her sweet

content.

COMPENSATION.

We love the flowers for their own sweet sakes,
And music joy inherent only wakes ;
Time brings no more, O darling ! than he takes.

It matters little to the river deep
If skies do smile or frown, or even weep ;
And love alone can love, or win, or keep.

To him who has a well-spring of delight
Within his bosom comes no bitter blight ;
The King of Day shuns not the Queen of Night.

He is not rich who never suffered loss ;
Nor saddest life that meekly bears its cross ;
And truth is sweet, though barren of all gloss.

" The kingdom is within you," not without ;

To him who trusts there is not any doubt ;

And Love's calm front can put dark Hate to rout.

LITTLE PHIL.

―――

"Make me a head-board, mister, smooth and painted;
you see,

Our ma she died last winter, and sister and Jack
and me

Last Sunday could hardly find her, so many new
graves about,

And Bud cried out, 'We 've lost her,' when Jack
gave a little shout.

We have worked and saved all winter—been hungry sometimes, I own—

But, we hid this much from father under the old
door-stone.

He never goes there to see her ; he hated her ;
scolded Jack

When he heard us talking about her and wishing
that she 'd come back.

But up in the garret we whisper, and have a good
time to cry,—

Our beautiful mother who kissed us, and was n't
afraid to die.

Put on it that she was forty, in November she went
away,

That she was the best of mothers, and we have n't
forgot to pray ;

And we mean to do as she taught us—be loving
and true and square,

To work and read, to love her, till we go to her up
there.

Let the board be white, like mother" (the small
chin quivered here,

And the lad coughed something under, and con-
quered a rebel tear.)

" Here is all we could keep from father, a dollar
and thirty cents,

The rest he has got for coal and flour, and partly
    to pay the rents."

Blushing the white lie over, and dropping the hon-
    est eyes :

"What is the price of head-boards, with writing and
    handsome size?"

"Three dollars!"—a young roe wounded just falls
    with a moan, and he,

With a face like the ghost of his mother, sank down
    on his tattered knee :

"Three dollars? and we shall lose her, next winter,
    —the graves and snow!"

But the boss had his arms about him, and cuddled
    the head of tow

Close up to the great heart's shelter, and womanly
    tears fell fast :

"Dear boy, you never shall lose her. O cling to
    your sacred past !

Come to-morrow, and bring your sister and Jack,
    and the board shall be

The best that this shop can furnish,—then come
    here and live with me."

When the orphans loaded their treasure on the
    rugged old cart next day,

The surprise of a foot-board varnish, with all that
    their love could say :

And "Edith St. John, our Mother!" baby Jack
    gave his little shout ;

And Bud, like a mountain daisy, went dancing her
    doll about ;

But Phil grew white and trembled, and close to the
    boss he crept,

Kissing him like a woman, shivered and laughed
    ⁓ and wept ;

"Do you think, my benefactor, in Heaven that
    she 'll be glad ?"

"Not so glad as you are, Philip ; but finish this job,
    my lad."

SURVIVAL.

———

"Alas," one said, "your garden sweets will live
To lure the butterfly, gay bird, and bee,
When you, dear heart, have found the unknown sea,
Whence no returning ship can tidings give
Of blissful voyagers."   "Nay, bless God 't is so,
That this enchantment lingers when I go !
Sing, golden birds, to every summer's rose,
And flutter, dappled streamers, in the sun !
Sick hearts will hail the beauty and repose
Of all these hands have gladly, fondly done.
Come always from the city's noise and heat ;
Take of true life renewed and happy lease.
Not face to face, but soul to soul we meet ;
The past idealized, the future peace."

COULD WE BUT KNOW !

Could we but know the substance from the shadow,

  Behold the subtle process of the mind,

The lights, the glooms, like cloud-rifts o'er a meadow,

  If only Faith were not so weak and blind !

If underneath the smile, the glamour weaving

  That gold-shot fabric—our own heart's desires—

Could we but know the truth, nor self-deceiving,

  Feed high the incense of Love's altar fires ;—

If our own souls were but the magic mirrors

  Reflecting all the beautiful, the pure ;

Detecting fraud, yet pitiful of errors,

  Still Love and Faith, transcendent, might endure.

But life has worn tear-channels in the spirit,

  And wrong and sorrow cruel doubts have nursed ;

The new-born king, alas ! he must inherit

    The pain, if all the splendor of the first !

Alas ! with eyes we see not, grope and falter,

    And miss the sunshine in the way we go ;

Reject the gold, with dross and tinsel palter,—

    Yet Heaven is near us, if we could but know.

THEODORE PARKER.

If we who never looked upon our friend,

Or heard the voice in holy counsel sweet

That set the world's great heart to love's soft beat,

With trembling eagerness our mite would send,

(Yet knowing that such life can never end,)

With what devotion will the hands he prest

Shower grateful tribute on their leader's rest !

He man and truth unfaltering did defend,

Breathing warm life into a dying faith ;

Reversing the grim order of " the blood,"

Cried : " Lo ! redemption in a perfect life !

A Saviour only in unending good ! "

Gave smiling challenge unto gentle Death ;

His heaven hath in hush of human strife.

EMERSON.

Never alone again, since I have found
The treasure of the jewels of thy mind—
Richer than Ormus, or the fairest bound
Of Persian beauty poets joy to find !
Do I behold the starry realms above,
Or walk the fields, or in the forest lie,
Thy matchless thoughts all loveliness approve ;
The winds repeat them in each passing sigh,
Birds sing thy messages of truth and praise,
The ferns repeat thy wisdom to the flowers,
The river murmurs of thy soul's calm ways
Beyond the mists that cloud our feeble powers !
And life, love, duty, by thy royal side,—
All things, O sage through thee are glorified !

WENDELL PHILLIPS.

AT SEVENTY YEARS.

Seventy ! thy winter has the air of June

When apple blossoms have displaced the snow ;

The heart of youth in thy blue eyes aglow,

And thy great spirit like the magic rune,

The key heroic that has set the tune

To man's enfranchisement from bonds and woe,

And woman's grand advancement.   If to know

Time's mighty secrets ; to enrich and prune

The lusty growths of this auspicious age ;

To sound such thrilling notes as never Pan

Piped in Arcadia, lover true of man !—

Not to have heard thee, were fate's irony ;

And having seen thy soul's illumined page,

Who is not hence thy loyal votary ?

TO PETER COOPER.

ON HIS NINETY-SECOND BIRTHDAY.

How manhood redeemeth his promise to pay

In the gold of the sunset illuming his day !

No counterfeit here,—not a grain of alloy !

Past ninety, you say ?   He is only a boy !

Heart of oak, sound to core, with a garland of

snows,

Life's juices like wine, aye, as red as the rose

That runs up the signal of summer to-night,

From his heart to his cheek, putting winter to

flight.

The gods of the Greeks had their temples ; and he

Is shrined in the temple he reared to the free,

In the hearts he has blessed, in the lives he has set

To the psalm of true living they cannot forget ;

And his praises are sung in the click of the wire,

The ring of the chisel, the crucible's fire ;

The canvas reveals him, the press will acclaim

The type he has set for the annals of fame.

I stood by the altars to Labor he reared ;

The incense of love to the God he revered

Was the breath of young lips in the eager pursuit

Of the good and the great—ah ! the coveted fruit

Never reached, but his wise and beneficent hand

Had lowered the bough ; gentle lord of the land,

Golden apples he gave, toiling millions to feed,

And we measure the man by the measureless deed.

Again I beheld, through the mist of my tears,

This soul in white raiment of beautiful years.

The man whose calm life was like rivers that flow

The deeper and purer that silent below

The broad channel holds its glad way to the sea

Of the infinite love ; happy toiler is he,

For we reap as we sow ; noble effort and aim

Have crowned him with honor and hallowed his
name.

When the even has come the good farmer looks
back

If his furrows are deep, in unvarying track ;

To his vision bright blades, silken banners in line

Are waving, of harvest rich promise and sign.

And our Peter the Great, in reviewing his past,

By the straight lines of duty finds blessing at last.

Nay, the flowers that spring from the footsteps of
care

More fragrant than lilies the idler may wear.

Long live ! noble builder to all that is best,

Oh late bloom the lily that shadows thy rest !

Flag of truce Death shall fling from his shallop of

    gold

As you drift to the land where love never grows

    old.

For the ships that put out from the Beautiful Isles,

Are fanned by the angels and freighted with smiles.

Lo, the harbor is calm, and its Master divine :

His rates are all just upon thine and on mine.

NAMING THE FLOWER.

TO F. L.

Nay, breathe not my name to your yacht or white
    steed,
Your hunter or falcon, but grant me to read
My name in the glorious song that was born
On your lips, with the sea in your soul, yestermorn ;
That study in clouds that you sketched at Glen-
    coe,—
Those drifts in the moonlight are whiter than snow ;
Let me see my initials above your last gem,—
I admire it, if all the cross critics condemn ;
Or if, of all loveliest things you would dower
With the name of your friend, may I live in a
    flower !

The song and the picture, the fair flowing line,

Are music, and beauty, and life.   How divine

To dwell in the arts, to inhabit a rose

Like the sea-haunted shell ! what enchanting repose

To sleep in the pearl-crusted, odorous cell

Of the wind-shaken, cream-tinted, luminous bell,

Awake to the tale the bright humming-bird sings,

Entranced by his eyes, and beguiled by his wings,

That weave their swift spells over vision and brain,

Until sound is a rainbow, half bliss and half pain !

Let me reign in the heart of the queen of the
    fair,—

In her robes of the samite the angels may wear,—

And learn the sweet secrets the hermit thrush told

When the red moon had turned all her tear-drops
    to gold,

And the fountain was silent with envy, and they

(The poor faded loves of the passionate day)

Were dying around her.   O rose of the South !

Let me dream, let me die on her tremulous mouth !

For the soul of the rose is the life she has brought

From Eden to bloom in a poet's clear thought.

The blush, the rich lustre, the veinings we trace,

Of the earth are they earthy ?—immortal the race !

No rose that is perfect dies out of the world.

Will the star that you love from its orbit be hurled ?

Roses live in the heart, though the heart may forget

The face of a lover ; they sharpen regret,

They consecrate joy, they dissolve in soft rain ;

They breathe in the young mother's lullaby strain ;

They felt the pure touch of the Master and smiled,

" And of such is the kingdom," the rose and the
     child.

They kindle the roseate tint of the cheek,

And laugh in the dimple confessions bespeak ;

They kiss the cold fingers when kissing is past

For our lips that must hunger in vain to the last.

Then wait until summer has burgeoned to flame,

And the rose of your sowing shall ask for her name.

With dew-drops the sunrise has reddened to wine,

Baptize this Canadian new namesake of mine ;—

Speak low, lest the blight of my sorrow shall close

Like death round the heart of your beautiful rose.

RELUCTANCE.

I marvel much that dying eyes should turn
    Regretfully on the imperilled way,
        The road once travelled ; e'en its scattered
        flowers
    Or cool white stones marking some happy day ;
Why shrink from shadow of a simple urn ?
        (Goal of the journey, this forced march of ours)
If crowned with roses or with wayside weeds,
    Why weeping falter in the song that ends
        In trembling pathos, howsoe'er it ranged,
    Without encore from any of the friends
Who praise or blame our good or evil deeds,
        Whose constancy no errors have estranged ?
Their loving hands our falling curtains stay,

And like as wayward children closer cling,

    Unto the gentle bosom that they wound,

  We seek the shelter of love's tender wing,

When fall the dews of life's departing day,

    Nor fear to stray beyond sweet mercy's bound.

WITH A SEA-SHELL.

" Our ship was like a painted ship
Upon a painted ocean."—COLERIDGE.

God send thy good ships all to thee,
    The white-winged messengers that swept
O'er fancy's fair and shoreless sea,
    The gallant ships where sunbeams slept.

Where never tempest dark and dread
    Careered, or lightning's lurid glare
Menaced thy lovely drooping head,
    Like flowers that bend in silent prayer.

Come ships full freighted with the stores
    Of India's sandal-wood and gems,

The shining fabrics of the shores
   That hoard the Old World's diadems ;

The perfumes caught from roses pressed
   In trembling joy by dying hands ;
Or pearls some Naiad love has blessed,
   Has dreaming strewn on golden sands.

Oh, flying ships that kiss the waves,
   Sail on around this changing world,
Bring hope and peace to all the graves
   Where Faith her dewy pinions furled !

Oh, bear to her a woman's thought,
   Bring truth and love and length of days,
The sweet content by patience wrought,
   The deeds that have no need of praise !

RED ROSES.

Let not the drifted snow of lilies white

    Press my dead heart, but roses red as flame ;

It will be morning then ; the stormy night

    Gone like the discords of some martial strain

Heard all too near—in the dim distance sweet.

    O rose of life ! that struggled to the light,

At last unfolding, beautiful, complete,

    To bud and bloom forever in His sight !

ORIENT.

———

They tell the heart 's hushed secret in a Rose,

And with an unclosed bud lovers reveal

The passion pure and ardent, that yet glows

The brighter with all efforts to conceal.

REMEMBER ME.

Remember me,—not for my eyes or voice,

    Or the old charm you found in smile or air,

    Or sunny tints you loved in my dark hair,

Or any word that bade you to rejoice,

Or aught, my darling, in which you have choice ;

    But for the memories that still must be

    The soul of life,—for these remember me.

TO A GIRL WITH A WATER-LILY.

But yesterday this peerless thing,
  A swaying censer in the light
Of crystal wave and glancing wing,
  Made the St. Lawrence white.
I marked it from the old canoe,
  The fairest of the fleet,
"And only, Golden Hair, for you,"
  I said, "this prize is meet.
Pirate of that enchanted sea
I bring my spoils, sweetheart, to thee!"

O bending skies of amethyst!
  O river grand! I dare
To turn again, O Time, and list
  The whispered vow and prayer;

To live again that royal hour
    That drained life's golden wine,
That left me neither wish nor power
    To win and wear the vine ;
A dreamer drifting with the tide,
With smiling front of maiden pride.

Could we have known, my love and I,
    How many lovely moons would kiss
The lilies in this mimic sky,
    How much the heart may miss,
Yet bravely o'er the tide of tears
    The circling waves of light uphold
A snowy banner changing years
    Have starred with hearts of gold,
We had not murmured !   Dear one, see !
Emblem of peace I give to thee.

LOST.

The barren moor, the forest dark,
  Gray frowning cliffs and blackened sky,
The still, deep lake—a plunge—and hark !
  Was that the bittern's mournful cry
  From out the stately rushes nigh ?

How wails the wind ! and something white
  A moment drifts the lilies by ;
Are angels upon guard to-night ?
  Hark ! once again the bittern's cry
  Among the rushes stark and high.

A maiden's footstep in the sand—
  A scarf, with dainty glove near by—
Ah, well ! the white and perfect hand,

With rival lilies it will lie !—

Was that the bittern's warning cry ?

O love ! how sweet (e'en unto death)

At that weird hour the rushes sigh !

The night wind softly holds its breath

To hear, perchance, the bittern's cry—

Then murmurs : " Love, betrayed, must die ! "

TWO LITTLE GRAVES.

Side by side two tiny hillocks, just as little lambs
　　may meet,
That have wandered from the fallows to the daisied
　·meadows sweet,
Sleeping in the blessed sunshine, hearing not the
　　mother's bleat.

One was borne to peaceful slumber when the sun-
　　set's crimson dyes
On her catafalque of lilies fell in royal draperies,
And a train of stately mourners looked farewell with
　　tearless eyes.

And I seemed to hear the mother, who had crossed
　　the silent sea

To await that angel-voyager in her snow-white
argosy,

Cry, Hosanna! to the Saviour, once a babe in
Galilee.

But the other, in the dawning of a bitter April day,

When the frozen tears of heaven on the pale arbutus
lay,

Was borne out in pauper's coffin by the sexton,
stern and gray.

Never glow of bud or leaflet on that little sinless
breast;

Never toll of bell, or chanting blessèd words of holy
rest,—

Only sobs of mortal anguish of a sinner unconfessed.

Not a meeting, but a parting; mother still, though
never wed;

And a haunting face beside her, looking down upon
  their dead,—
O beguiling face, and craven ! " Thou dost judge
  him, God ! " she said.

" If I dare not look the way she went for keen re-
  morse, O Lord !
What of him who lured me onward by distortion of
  Thy word ?
Yet for him the world has honors, and for me the
  flaming sword ! "

But He hears who heeds the sparrows, who hath
  justice for us all ;
Both the lambs within His bosom, is he deaf to
  spirit call ?
Nay ; His arm of sweet compassion—it will break
  the woman's fall.

IN REMEMBRANCE.

―――――

M. E. T.

If sunbeams could be held and braided
   Within the meshes of her hair,
If orient pearls by rosebuds shaded
   Had made her cheeks so softly fair,
If violets could smile serenely
   As did her shining eyes—to me
The secret of her beauty queenly
   No more a mystery would be.

If you have plucked the scented clover,
   And drank the sweets of white and red,
Perhaps they breathed the story over
   Of all her sweeter lips have said.

If you have heard the song of thrushes

From summer meadows borne along,

Perhaps those clear, melodious gushes,

Repeat the gladness of her song.

Thou source of beauty, joy, and blessing,

Who hast to thine own realms of love

Removed from our too fond caressing

This darling flower, to bloom above,—

We thank Thee that in thousand phases

These hints and tokens Thou hast given,

That we may keep her earthly graces,

And dream of what she is in Heaven.

THE BROOK.

Two streams divide the little town
    Where I abide, and one
Is dusk beneath the hazel's brown,
    And silver in the sun.

God never made a purer thing,
    Or one more glad, I know,
And always in the happy spring,
    When fires of sunset glow,

I seek the comfort of its face,
    The music of its voice ;
And in my mossy hiding-place
    With nature I rejoice.

The alders dip their tassels red

   Where minnows love to sport,

And in the willows overhead

   Loquacious martins court.

Afar the lowing of the herd,

   The little ones at play,

The distant bell, or song of bird,

   The hush of dying day ;

Low sighing of the solemn wind,

   Soft ripple of the waves,

Remembered melodies that find

   Their way among the graves.

Where tiny brave anemones

   And nun-like violet,

Lost in such saintly reverie

   Of love and vain regret,

That woven with sweet eglantine,
  Our human tenderness
Dear vanished faces can define,
  With not a smile the less.

And often when the blessèd rain
  Has overflowed the brook,
I hear my baby coo again
  From out the ferny nook.

Then, if a fleecy cloud is borne
  Along this mirror fair,
I say it is the raiment worn
  By beings of the air.

Oft when the golden nets are cast
  Adown the azure deep,
I see a white sail drifting past,
  Stretch out my arms and weep.

As starving castaway may cry

    To homeward bark in vain :

I hail the life-boat drawing nigh

    To rescue from all pain.

Thus nature keepeth sacrament,

    And folds us in embrace ;

So tender and beneficent

    We see our Father's face.

O mothers ! if ye only knew

    How the white raiment of your prayers

Clings to the soul, when lost to view

    The splendid robes the body wears,—

The children might be clothed upon

With light like His, the Holy One !

THE GRAVE.

The grave is cruel ; for it bars the deed
  Of latent mercy, presses down the scale
Of justice with a miser's hungry greed—
  'Gainst frozen hearts what can our tears avail ?

The grave is silent ; answer it has none,
  Although you cry repentant till you faint—
Always beneath the cold, accusing stone
  Lieth a shrined and consecrated saint.

The grave is mighty ; 'gainst it your appeal
  Beats like the surges on the flinty rock ;
The pleading bosom pressing tempered steel
  Hath only wounds and anguish for the shock.

The grave is rich ; your dearest treasures lie
　Shut from your longing—hair of beaten gold,
The ruby lips, the sapphire beaming eye,
　Pearls fair and perfect as the sea-kings hold.

The grave is patient ; flowers come and go,
　The robins wait expectant every spring
To herald any protest from below
　Against the charges that the world may bring.

The grave is just ; for always, soon or late,
　The exile cometh to his own again,
For time reverses false decrees of fate—
　The martyr liveth, loved of gods and men.

The grave 's a haven for the sorrow-crost—
　How calm they sleep who enter into rest !
What if they find the dreams they weeping lost,
　The real life—and wake divinely blest !

The grave is constant ; it will fail you not
　　Though friends forsake and fortune from you
　　　　flies—
Honors elude—one little sheltered spot
　　Hath soft, cool grasses for your tired eyes.

The grave—I marvel we should fear to go
　　Where one by one the dear ones passed from
　　　　sight.
Our hands are in the Father's, and we know
　　His love is 'round us, be it day or night.

A NOCTURNE.

To-night fair Venus to her breast
Such shield of woven amethyst
And flaming rubies, opals, prest,
That all the vast star-studded west—
    A sea of fire—

Rolled in great waves of wondrous light,
Too radiant for mortal sight;
The new-born moon, a-tremble, white,
As tender babes that shrink in fright
    When lights expire;

And Mars, red orb fair swinging free,
Revealing snowy poles and sea
Of azure; all immensity

Pervaded with sweet harmony ;

    Soul mounting higher,

I heard the vibrant chords of those

Great hearts that sang as sings the rose,

When first its passionless repose

Is broken by the song that glows

    With pained desire,—

Until, like cymbals clashing clear,

Each lovely flashing, singing sphere

The secrets of its changing year

Disclosing to the spirit's ear,

    The mighty lyre

Of nature, smote by minstrels old,

The sons of God, as sages told,

With trailing robes of gems and gold,

From world to world grand peans rolled

    Forever nigher !

All the great masters slowly beat

The measure of Love's nocturne sweet,

While severed hearts like lilies meet

On crystal tides, in murmurs greet

　　The starry pyre

That kindles with divinest flame,

Responsive to each sacred name

That holds the threefold blessèd claim

Of music's chosen, in the fane

　　Of God, our Sire !

But over all the notes that stirred

The deeps, that e'en Nirvana heard,

There every lost and happy bird

Awoke to learn and voiced in word

　　Aspire ! aspire !

Oh, sweeter than all waters wild,

Or winds that whisper low and mild,

Or prayers beside the undefiled,

His liquid notes the little child,—

Too soon to tire

Of discords that this low estate

Yields jarringly to souls elate

With echoes of the blessèd fate

Immortals chant, beyond the gate

Of Death how dire !—

Our angel sang, as sing shall these

Bright sisters, fairest Pleiades,

As seraphs sound the mysteries

Of our transcendent destinies

With lips of fire !

And ever from the starry space

The beautiful young music face,

Her wooing, winning, flowery grace,

Still drew me on to blest embrace,—

　　O lost desire !

This " song of songs " rang out, like bells

In dreams, from fragrant lily cells :

" Who seeketh Mercy's holy wells

Hath peace that earthly joy excels,

　　As harps of wire

" Attuned to hallowed keys that keep

True time with Nature, pure and deep ;

O mothers ! smile ! but never weep

For those our Father's love shall keep

　　From sin's black mire ! "

THE END

www.ingramcontent.com/pod-product-compliance
Lightning Source LLC
Chambersburg PA
CBHW022355020726

47500CB00002B/291